Hank Hammer

by Adria Klein   illustrated by Andy Rowland

Sammy Saw

Sophie Screwdriver

Today is the big contest. Hank is
very excited! He jumps out of bed.

He brushes his teeth and gets ready.

"Have a fun day," his mom says.
"Good luck at the contest."

"Thanks, Mom," Hank says as he rushes out the door.

"Hi, everyone! Are you ready for the big contest?" asks Hank.

"We're ready!" they yell.

"I have the wood," says Sammy.

"I have the nails," says Tia.

"I have the red paint and the blue paint," says Sophie.

"And I have the plans," says Hank.

"We are going to build the best birdhouse!" says Sammy.

"It's time to start," says Sophie.

"What do we do?" asks Tia.

"Just follow my plan," says Hank.
"I have everything mapped out
right here."

"First, we measure everything," says Hank.

"That's my job," says Tia.

"Great!" says Hank.

"Next, we cut the wood,"
says Hank.

"That's my job," says Sammy.

"Great!" says Hank.

"Then, we put the house together," says Hank.

"I'll hold the nails. You can pound them in," says Sophie.

"Great!" says Hank.

"Now we paint it," says Hank.

"We can all do that," says Sophie.

"Great!" says Hank.

The birdhouse is done. The tool team sets it on the table next to the other ones.

"It's perfect," says Hank.

"I think we built the best one,"
says Sammy.

"And we did it together," says Tia.

"I have one more thing to add,"
says Hank.

"Now it's perfect," says Sammy.

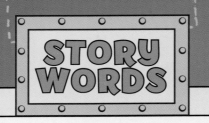

STORY WORDS

contest   birdhouse

measure   follow

build   together

Total Word Count: **241**

STONE ARCH **READERS** LEVEL 2
TOOL SCHOOL
Sophie Screwdriver

STONE ARCH **READERS** LEVEL 2
TOOL SCHOOL
Tia Tape Measure

STONE ARCH **READERS** LEVEL 2
TOOL SCHOOL
Sammy Saw

TOOL SCHOOL